Basil Bat's Be...

written and illustrated by
Heather S Buchanan

edited by Nina Filipek
designed by Liz Auger

Copyright © 1995 Heather S Buchanan. All rights reserved.
Published in Great Britain by World International,
an imprint of Egmont Publishing Ltd., Egmont House, PO Box 111,
Great Ducie Street, Manchester M60 3BL.
Printed in Finland. ISBN 0 7498 2275 9

A catalogue record for this book is available from the British Library.

N

W   E

S

Basil Bat's branch

Rumpus Rabbit's burrow

Muzzy Mouse's house

Maurice Mole's hole

Scampa Squirrel's tree

Henrietta Hedgehog's log

Buttercup Meadow stretches from the Deep Dark Wood in the north, where Basil Bat and Scampa Squirrel live, to the small stream in the south, where Maurice Mole has his home.

Henrietta Hedgehog lives in an old log on the east side, and Muzzy Mouse's straw house is under the hedge to the west. In the middle of the meadow lives Rumpus Rabbit.

This is Basil's story...

B asil Bat was in a mood. He felt cross about everything. He didn't know why he felt so cross, but the real reason was very simple. Basil was terribly tired.

It was the end of the summer, and the days and nights were becoming chilly. So when Basil hung upside-down on his branch to sleep, as bats usually do, his toes got colder and colder. When they were so numb that they couldn't feel the branch any more, they lost their grip and the poor sleeping bat suddenly plummeted down, waking with a start when he hit the forest floor.

S campa Squirrel, who lived in a tree near to Basil's in the Deep Dark Wood, often heard Basil land with a yell, and she felt very sorry for him. She tried to talk to him, but he was too cross to listen.

"The trouble with you, Basil, is that you are over tired, and that makes you feel cross," explained Scampa.

"No I'm not," huffed Basil, and he flew off again.

"Basil needs to be warm whilst he sleeps," Scampa suggested to Maurice Mole. "He isn't his old cheerful self at the moment, poor thing. It's all because his feet get so cold. Whatever can we do to help?"

"Make him some bedsocks!" said Maurice, at once.

"Of course! That's the answer," smiled Scampa, delighted with the idea.

S campa set off straight away to see Henrietta in her log house. The hedgehog was always busy knitting something for someone.

"Just get me the wool," said Henrietta, "and I'll make them at once. It's a very good idea."

Rumpus Rabbit was keen to help, so he was sent round the field next to Buttercup Meadow to collect the bits of wool that the sheep had left behind caught on the brambles. He washed it all in the stream and enjoyed getting very wet himself at the same time!

B ack at Henrietta's house, the hedgehog got her knitting needles out, and her little wooden spindle.

"Stripy socks would really suit Basil," suggested the hedgehog thoughtfully.

So Muzzy Mouse, who lived by the blackberry hedge, kindly collected the last of the year's berries and squashed them into juice in a conker shell. Just as the little mouse was dipping half the soft white wool into the deep pinky-mauve liquid, Basil flew down and rudely helped himself to a drink of the blackberry juice.

"Don't drink that, Basil!" squeaked Muzzy. "We are using it to dye the socks Henrietta is making for you, to keep your feet warm at night." Muzzy was so excited and happy about their plan she couldn't resist telling him.

"Well you needn't bother, because I'm not wearing any stupid socks!" spluttered Basil. "Whatever would a bat look like in socks!"

Then he flew away, leaving Muzzy feeling very disappointed.

R umpus Rabbit was not upset. "Don't worry," he said. "He'll change his mind when he sees them. Let's carry on."

So the animals finished dyeing the wool. Then they washed it, and dried it, and Scampa spun it out into a long yarn on Henrietta's spindle. Henrietta wound it into a ball, and at last began to knit.

Mole was worried that the socks would slip off when Basil was flying, so Muzzy made strings with pom-poms at the ends, to tie them on with.

Whilst the animals were busy making his socks, Basil was still flying around on his own, feeling very cross. He was cross because he was tired, but he was even more cross with himself because he knew he'd been really horrid to his friends, and he was afraid they wouldn't like him any more. If he could have gone back to say sorry he would have felt better at once, but he felt too cross even to do that. Poor Basil!

At last the socks were ready! They looked really wonderful. The pom-poms made the perfect finishing touch. The animals were very pleased with them. But they still didn't know whether Basil would like them, let alone agree to wear them.

Scampa wrapped them up carefully and they all set out to show them to their friend, to ask him to try them and see if they would warm his poor cold feet.

The animals searched until sunset but they couldn't find Basil Bat anywhere. They went into the Deep Dark Wood and shouted up to his pine tree, but he wasn't there. They went back through Buttercup Meadow to the stream but he wasn't there. They even searched the blackberry hedge, but he wasn't there either. He wasn't in any of the places they would have expected him to be and they were getting rather anxious about him.

At last when they were just about to give up and go home, Mole spotted Basil's toes sticking out of the daisies behind a molehill, and realised he was asleep.

"He's here! Quick, bring the socks!" he whispered to the others.

They eased the beautiful, warm, woolly, stripy socks on to the sleeping Basil and, without waking him, tied the pom-poms at the top.

"Oh, I do hope he likes them…" sighed Muzzy, as they all crept away to hide and keep watch.

B asil slept soundly all night, for the first time in ages. Once the socks were on his feet, a dreamy smile crept on to his sleeping face and as he grew warmer, he snored in a happy, stretched-out sort of way.

He awoke with the dawn, and the first thing he saw, to his great surprise, was a pair of pink and white, woolly, stripy feet. He thought he was still dreaming. He flew around in circles, but the new feet stayed with him. Then he noticed his friends watching him. So he called down to them, "Thank you! I'll never ever take them off!"

B asil had slept well, so he wasn't feeling cross any more – he was his old happy self again. The animals were delighted. Henrietta offered to make him a spare pair of socks so he could change them now and again! Best of all, Basil realised that real friends are friends for ever, because they always understand you, even when you get bad-tempered, and they try to help you to feel better. Besides, he looked very handsome in his pink and white socks!

The End

TITLES IN THE BUTTERCUP MEADOW SERIES
BY HEATHER S BUCHANAN

RUMPUS RABBIT
HENRIETTA HEDGEHOG
MAURICE MOLE
SCAMPA SQUIRREL
BASIL BAT
MUZZY MOUSE